P9-CER-251

lauren child

I Will Never NOT EVER Eat a Tomato

CANDLEWICK PRESS
CAMBRIDGE, MASSACHUSETTS

This book is for Soren

who is crazy about tomatoes

but would never eat a baked bean

with love from Lauren

who is keen on Marmite

but would rather not eat a raisin

Copyright © 2000 by Lauren Child

All rights reserved.

First U.S. edition 2000

Library of Congress Cataloging-in-Publication Data is available.

Library of Congress Catalog Card Number 99-057573

This book was typeset in Officina Serif Book and Badloc.

First published in Great Britain in 2000 by Orchard Books, London

The illustrations were done in mixed media.

Candlewick Press, 2067 Massachusetts Avenue, Cambridge, Massachusetts 02140

Designed by Anna-Louise Billson

ISBN 0-7636-1188-3

1 2 3 4 5 6 7 8 9 10

Printed in Singapore

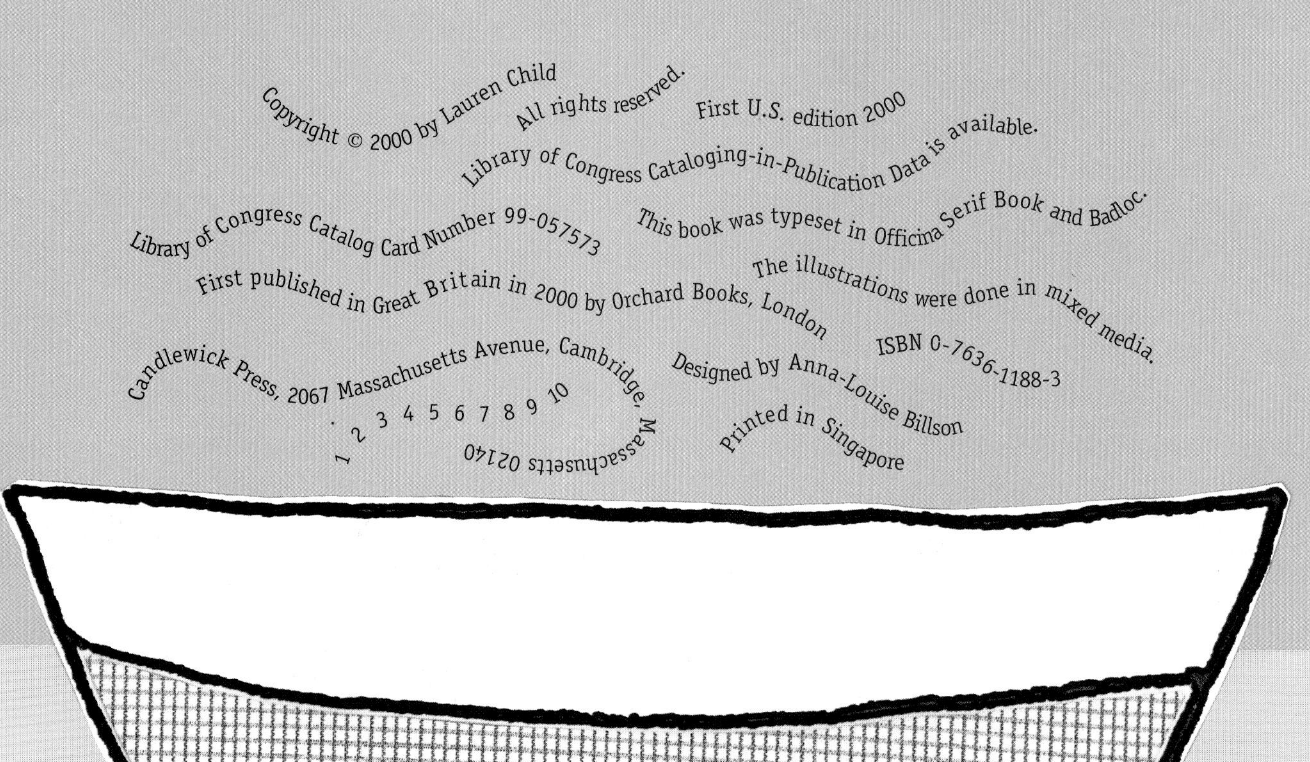

I have this little sister, Lola.
She is small and very funny.
Sometimes I have to keep an eye on her.
Sometimes Mom and Dad ask me to give Lola her dinner.
This is difficult because she is a very fussy eater.

Lola won't eat carrots, of course.
She says carrots are for rabbits.

I say, "What about peas?"

Lola says,
"Peas are too small
and too green."
One day I played a good trick on her.

Lola was sitting at the table,
waiting for her dinner.
And she said,
"I do not eat

peas or carrots or potatoes

or mushrooms or spaghetti

or eggs

or sausages.

I do not eat

cauliflower or cabbage or baked beans

or bananas or oranges.

And I am not fond of

apples or rice or cheese

or

fish sticks.

And

I absolutely

will never

not ever

eat a tomato." (My sister hates tomatoes.)

And I said,
"That is lucky

because we are not having any of those things.

We are not going to eat any peas or carrots
or potatoes or mushrooms or spaghetti or eggs or sausages.

There will be no cauliflower or
cabbage or baked beans or bananas or oranges.

We don't have any apples or
rice or cheese or fish sticks
and certainly
no tomatoes."

Lola looked at the table.

"Then why are those carrots there, Charlie?

I
don't
ever
eat
carrots."

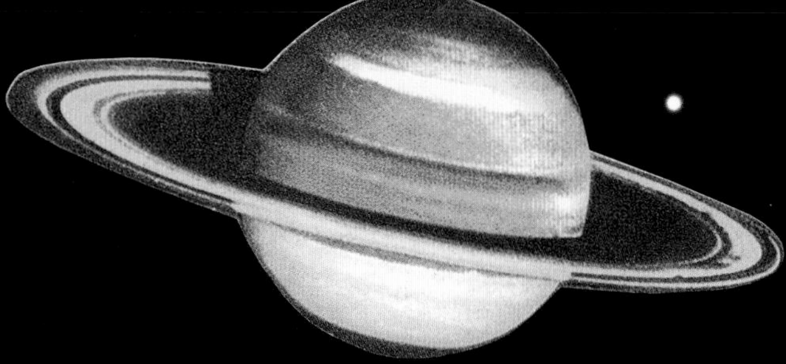

And I said,
"Oh, you think these are carrots.
These are not carrots.
These are orange twiglets from Jupiter."

"They look just like carrots to me," said Lola.
"But how can they be carrots?" I said.
"Carrots don't grow on Jupiter."

"That's true," said Lola.
"Well, I might just try one
if they're all the way from Jupiter.
Mmm, not bad," she said, and took another bite.

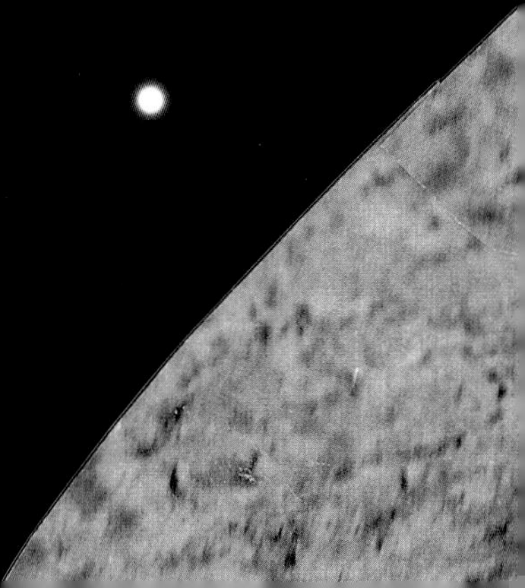

Then Lola saw some peas.

"I don't eat peas,"

said Lola.

I said,

"These are not peas.

Of course they are not.

These are green drops

from Greenland.

They are made

out of green

and fall from the sky."

"But I don't eat green

things," Lola said.

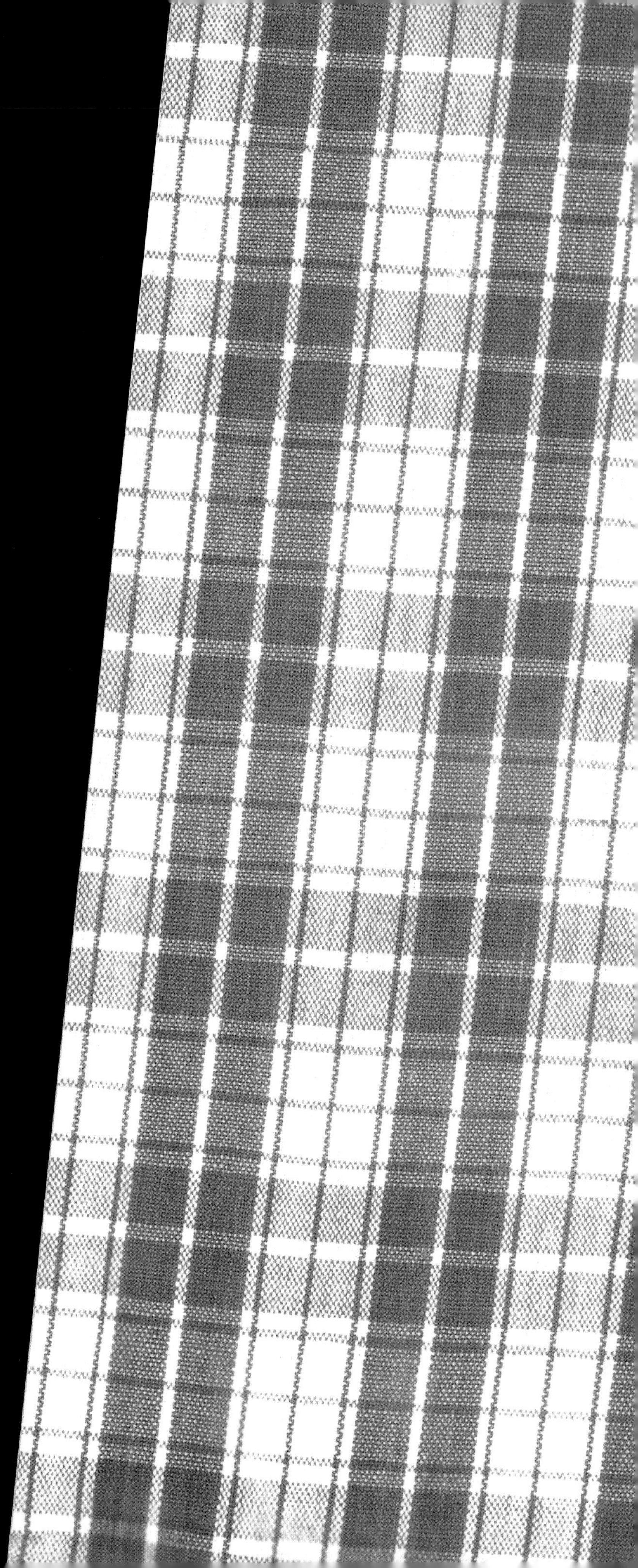

"Oh goody,"

I said.

"I'll have

your share.

Green drops

are so

incredibly

rare."

"Well,

maybe

I'll nibble

just one

or two.

Oh," said

Lola, "quite

tasty."

Next Lola saw the potato.
"I will not eat potato
so don't even try,
not even mashed."

“Oh,
this
isn’t
mashed potato.
People often
think that but no,
this is cloud fluff from
the pointiest peak of Mount Fuji.”
“Oh,” said Lola, “in that case a large helping for me.
I love to eat cloud.”

"Charlie,"
she said,
"those look like fish sticks to me,
and I would
never
eat a fish stick."

"I know that. These are not fish sticks.
These are ocean nibbles from the supermarket
under the sea — mermaids eat them all the time."

"Oh, I went to that supermarket
one time with Mom.
Yes, I know the ones.
I think I've had them before," Lola said, gobbling.
"Are there any more?"

And then she said,

"Charlie, will you pass me one of those?"

And I said,

"What, one of those?"

And Lola said,
"Yes, Charlie,
one of those."
And I couldn't believe my eyes
because guess what she was pointing at —
the **tomatoes**.

And I said,

"Are you sure?

Really?

One

of these?"

And she said,
"Yes, of course, moonsquirters are my favorite.

Charlie

"You didn't think they were
tomatoes,
did you, Charlie?"